I0566595

Tails of Reggie

By
Sarah Nade

Published by: Check Publications Inc.

29A Hartfield Road, Bexhill, East Sussex

TN39 3EA

ISBN: 978-1-9999782-1-1

Contents

Chapter One

Intros

Harry O'Brien and Reggie are relaxing on Harry's boat. It has been a long day where Harry has been planing, polishing and varnishing different pieces of wood on the boat. Now they can hear the lapping of the water as they sink into the padded seats at the helm and Harry pours his first tipple of the evening.

"This is the life" thinks Harry as he quaffs his first mouthful of Merlot and sighs with an air of satisfaction that comes from having done a good day's work.

"Cheers Reggie!"

"Harry!" comes the call, "food's on the table, head on in."

The hail is from Clair O'Brien, Harry's other half. Their garden backs onto the shoreline where Harry's boat is moored.

"I'll have to go Reggie, look after things." And with a rueful smile Harry climbs down the small ladder at the side of the boat clutching his glass of Merlot. Reggie is meeting his daughter Lucy that evening so isn't put out by Harry's untimely exit. He scrambles off the boat as it is still on dry land. The tide is coming in and soon it will be harder to disembark.

When Lucy arrives by the shore Reggie suggests that they go for a ramble by the sea. As they make their way a huge wave descends upon the beach.

"Run for cover!" Shouts Reggie and pulls Lucy to safety. The wave crashes down with an almighty bang just to the side of their ombrifuge.

"Another two centimetres and we'd have been like a couple of drowned rats" comments Lucy, and they both look at each other and burst out laughing.

~~~~~~~~~~~~~~~~~~~

Donal and Samantha Jones are in the estate agent's office looking through a list of properties.

"I like the one we viewed online" says Samantha, "let's ask to see it and maybe two others close by."

"Sounds like a plan" replies Donal who is glad to have the decision made for him. At that moment Cardew Bing, the local agent steps up to them brandishing papers.

"Good morning Mr and Mrs Jones" he enthuses, "can I be of service? May I call you by your Christian names? We're a friendly bunch down here in Bexhill." Before they have a chance to reply he fawns on: "I've noticed your names written on my notes; how do you pronounce your Christian name Mr Jones?"

"Its Donald without the D" says Donal quickly before Cardew can start again.

"Well Onald and Samantha, welcome to our neck of the woods, I'm confident we can find you the perfect property!"

Donal wants to correct him but after seeing Sam's withering expression decides against it.

"We've found a property we like online in Maple Walk. Could you show us that and maybe two others close by? asks Sam.

"It'll be my pleasure" retorts Cardew, "Maple Walk is only a short drive so we can start there first." The house is lined by six pollarded trees which look as if they are tipping their knobbly hats to the prospective buyers.

"It's a four bed property with double garage and lovely wrap around garden plus west facing patio for those sundowners on a perfect evening" enthuses Cardew. Just then Cardew's phone rings and he profusely excuses himself much to the relief of Donal and Sam, who can now explore uninterrupted.

"Let's start with the bedrooms and see which one could suit Jasmine" says Sam.

"Good idea" agrees Donal, "and maybe check the master suite first" he says with a glint in his eye.

"Ok Mr Truncheon, lead the way" replies Sam.

She always calls him this when he makes a naughty suggestion. After all he is a policeman, albeit a detective sergeant now, but he'd done his time on the beat when they'd lived in Hammersmith. They view the master bedroom and en suite bathroom with Sam managing to avoid Donal's tickling antics, and come to bedroom three which would probably be right for their daughter Jasmine.

"Oh this is lovely" says Sam, "we'll have to come back and bring Jazz to see this."

Cardew catches up with them as they tour the grounds and then takes them to look at two more local properties, but Donal and Sam really like that first house in Maple Walk.

Chapter Two

Reggie's close encounter

He can feel his heart thumping and can hear soft footsteps. There's someone else in the room. He can just make out a shadowy figure by the glow of moonlight filtering in from a chink in the curtains. He begins to edge towards the staircase to try and find a way out of the room but there are precious few hiding places. As he backs into the cupboard under the stairs, the shadowy figure must have heard a faint telltale scuttle and raises his arm. Lord Carrington holds the gun aloft and engages the barrels, takes aim and retorts:

"Got you, you pesky rat!" BANG! BANG! The silence is broken by the enormous sound of the shotgun and a piece of wood splinters from the under stairs cupboard.

Reggie decides the best line of defence is attack so runs straight at Lord Carrington who is desperately trying to reload. With an almighty bound Reggie jumps onto the table, uses the length of it as a runway, and launches himself through the air onto Lord Carrington's shoulder.

"What the deuce!" Shouts the Lord but Reggie's not stopping and with a single leap, he launches himself at the window which is just open at the top. Lord Carrington flings open the french windows shouting:

"Now I've got you, you pesky rat!"

"Henry!" Booms the voice of Lady Carrington "stop shooting at such small game! There's a perfectly good natural predator who will do the job for you if you'll turn out the lights and stop making such an infernal racket!"

As Lady Carrington switches off the lights and pulls Henry back into the drawing room of Barkley Hall, a swishing sound is heard. The owl descends on the garden at great speed and picks up Reggie with one talon. However Reggie is a lot heavier than the owl's normal fare so they only manage to bump along the grass and into a small ditch at the end of the lawn. Luckily out of sight of the stately occupants.

"Thanks Ollie" says a relieved Reggie, "you saved my bacon."

"Just thank your lucky stars that Aloysius is on parent duty tonight otherwise you'd have been on the spit roast by now feeding his four brood" replies Ollie.

"I owe you big time" says Reggie, "and I won't forget."

Chapter Three

House buying

The Jones family had booked up to revisit the house in Maple Walk and together they are now giving it a thorough viewing.

"This room is fantastic!" Cries Jasmine, "can I really have this one?"

"Of course Jazz" replies Sam, "it's the one we'd have picked for you."

Jasmine excitedly climbs onto the window seat and, crossing her legs in the Lotus position, begins to plan where everything will go. Donal and Sam move off to the other bedrooms and leave Jasmine to her musing.

"I'll make a deal with you Sam," says Donal "you can have bedroom four for your interior design projects, and we'll keep bedroom two for guests, which leaves me the study on the ground floor at the front. As you know I need a room that can be locked and made secure for the confidential information received from head office."

"I still don't understand why we have moved so far and why you've been given such a big bonus, but I'm sure you'll fill me in when you can" says Samantha.

"I certainly will" adds Donal, "but it's great having the money to make a downpayment on this house."

Detective Sergeant Donal Jones has been seconded from Scotland Yard by Hastings' CID to follow up on suspicions of a major import fraud in the Hastings' area. The case is so "hush hush" that Scotland Yard planned Donal's move to look like a semi-retirement package and a downgrade so as not to alert any suspicion, as they feel that someone high up in the force is involved. Hence his move to Bexhill.

Donal recalls that initially he was not happy about the move to the sleepy coastal town until his Chief brought him into the office and pointed out that his salary would be at Inspector level and all moving costs covered. After this interview Donal had pulled his arm down from behind his back and walked out with a smile on his face! He couldn't wait to tell Sam the good news.

Sam had always hated living in SW London: "Too crowded, too much pollution, too noisy and no real community; apart from that it's perfect!"

Donal knows that Sam wants to set up her own interior design business from home, and feels that there will be a great opportunity for this in Bexhill, especially as Jazz is now thirteen and becoming more independent. Although they do still enjoy shopping together, especially with Sam's credit card!

"We just need to visit the town hall and sign up for the council services" adds Donal. "Let's take Jazz with us and get everything done this morning, then we can have a celebratory lunch together."

"This is so exciting!" Replies Sam.

Chapter Four

Mr Potts the milkman

Reggie is riding, as he regularly does, on the milk float from Cooden Beach along Cooden Sea Road to Buckhurst Place to visit his daughter Lucy who lives with Pamela Potts; Mr Potts's cousin. Reggie as usual takes a drink by tipping one of the milk bottles on its side and scratching the top off with his paw and drinking as the milk pours out. He wonders why Mr Potts never kicks him off the cart but instead always blames himself for travelling too fast round the bend and knocking over the bottle. Reggie thinks Mr Potts must have a soft spot for him and he's very lucky!

Today Mr Potts keels over in Cooden Sea Road just as he's put a pint of milk down outside 'Tide's In' cottage.

"Oh my God" thinks Reggie, "he's having a heart attack and I can't do anything to help."

Just then he spots Johnny Gant taking Benjy, his pet sausage dog for their morning constitutional, but heading in the opposite direction.

"Think, think Reggie what can I do?" He muses and with a flash of inspiration, Reggie begins to run after the perambulating pair. Luckily Johnny has stopped to look at a robin chirping in the nearby tree so Reggie is able to catch up to them quickly. Benjy notices Reggie but doesn't seem keen to give chase and Johnny is still engrossed in his bird watching and listening. Reggie starts to put his front paws in his ears and stick his tongue out at Benjy.

"Thank God Johnny's not looking" thinks Reggie "He'd never believe it!" Still no joy from Benjy so Reggie pulls the most frightening face he can muster and makes a raspberry sound at Benjy and that's it! Benjy's had enough! He turns round and runs at Reggie until all his lead has been used. The lead is almost yanked from Johnny's grip as Benjy strains at the leash with dogged determination. At this point the lead clasp breaks, and with a triumphant yelp, Benjy's on the chase!

Johnny can't believe what he's seeing. A sausage dog chasing a rat almost the same size. He runs after Benjy, but stops momentarily to pick up a stick for protection. He knows rats can be pretty vicious if cornered. Reggie can hear Benjy's barks getting louder so he puts on a sprint until he reaches the garden of 'Tide's In' cottage. He can just see Benjy coming over the brow of the hill and hear Johnny calling after him so with a huge jump, he launches himself into a hawthorn hedge just on the other side of Mr Potts.

"Ouch, these prickles are sharp" mutters Reggie, "but at least it might keep Benjy at bay."

Reggie moves cautiously further into the bush as Benjy arrives still barking furiously. Johnny's puffing a bit from his unexpected exertions but as he approaches the cottage he can see the torso of Mr Potts.

"Heel!" Johnny says commandingly, and Benjy knows that tone and immediately stops barking and returns to Johnny's side.

"Good boy" says Johnny, taking a chew from his pocket and giving it to Benjy. Now he's at Mr Pott's side and taking out his phone, dials 999. Whilst doing this he turns to Mr Potts and begins singing to himself 'staying Alive' by the Bee Gees to obtain the right tempo for his cardiac resuscitation attempts.

Mr Potts is soon in the ambulance, going in and out of consciousness and whilst in this state overhears the paramedics:

"Johnny was saying that if his dog Benjy hadn't chased that rat back to where Mr Potts was lying, he might not have made it"

~~~~~~~~~~~~~~~~~~~~~~~~~~~~~

Mr Potts recovers and eventually returns to work. He now deliberately takes the Cooden Beach corner just a little too fast, so that one of the "gold top" milk bottles has to fall on it's side.

Chapter Five
Howl for the owl

Ollie is having a great evening. Perched on a branch of his favourite chestnut tree, watching and listening for the tell tale rustle of small rodents, or as he likes to describe them: 'dinner'. He's just nodding off on his favourite perch when he hears a rustle from behind. Suddenly a noose drops over his head and a strange but melodious voice regales:

"Got you my beauty." Ollie tries to fly upwards but the noose just tightens at each attempt, and then a large cloth is thrown over him and he's bodily lifted from the tree. He feels a sharp prick to his side and immediately begins to feel as if his wings and body don't belong to him, and he falls into a rather soporific state.

Waking up sometime later, Ollie sees a sign; 'Barkins' and he's on a very low perch outside of a garden centre and is being gazed at by strange people.

"Ooh Mummy, can I take one home? They're so cuddly" screeches one small person.

"They're not for sale" says the man with the melodious voice, "but you can buy some food from us which has been specially formulated to give the birds all the nutrients they need."

Ollie is fed up just sitting around all day and not being able to fly. He has plenty of time to ruminate on old acquaintances and friends. He recalls Victor the Vulture, whom he met at 'Bird World' in Tenterden, saying as he sits waiting for his next meal:

"Patience be damned, I'm gonna kill something!" Then of his friend Percy Pig who likes to call Ollie's Dad Aloysius: 'Owl who itches' and wishes he would f-f-f-fly away. Percy stutters when he's excited and all of Ollie's friends sing in response to his rather unkind jibe: "P-p-p Percy, oh please have mercy, don't give us a hard time, when we m- m-make fun of you" to the song of "p-p-pick up a penguin" from the TV ad of the same name.

At the end of a long and boring day just sitting tethered to his perch, Ollie is bundled up and taken in a van back to a huge open air room with thirty other birds. They are well fed but kept on perches for hours. The room is completely caged so they can fly for very short distances but it's very difficult to miss all the other birds trying to exercise in such a small space.

The man with the melodious voice is a Lithuanian named Ledmen. He genuinely loves the birds but does not understand how stressed they are. He takes some out in a field at the back of his cottage near Bexingham Manor but they are always kept on a very long trace so that he can train them to catch meat from his gloved hand. After many months the birds become so dependent on him that he can take them off the trace. He then uses them for demonstrations at local outdoor events.

Ollie hasn't had this induction yet and is dreading it. He would still like his freedom.

Chapter Six

Revelations at the Town Hall

Jasmine is looking a little forlorn as she waits in the big office at the town hall. She is taken pity on by Henrietta Lurch the secretary to the councillors.

"Hello" says Henrietta, "you've been here a long time, would you like to wait in the board room? There's a library in the corner of the room and there may be something of interest for you to read."

"Thanks a lot" says Jasmine with relief as she'd left her mobile in the car. As they enter the room there is a man sitting at the desk.

"Oh sorry" said Henrietta "Oh it's you Councillor Bond, sorry to disturb you but I suggested this young lady could have a look at the books."

"Come in, come in" chants Councillor Basil Bond, "you won't disturb me."

Henrietta turns to Jasmine and points to the chair by the bookshelves: "Sit here my dear and I'll let you know as soon as your parents have finished."

"Thanks" mutters Jasmine as she walks towards the book case. Henrietta leaves the room smiling broadly at the Councillor.

"Come over and sit by me" entices Basil as he turns towards her, rotating in his leather chair. "You're a very pretty girl, what's your name?"

"Jasmine" she says as she coyly ambles towards the councillor's chair keeping her gaze downward. She feels uncomfortable but doesn't know why. Reggie is perched on top of a collection of books in the bookcase which overlooks Basil's desk. He's just woken from a rather nice dream about Lucy and him eating a particularly good cheese.

"Red Leicester I think" he muses to himself but then seems to 'hear' another thought that is not his:

"Wish my Mum and Dad would hurry up" comes into Reggie's mind.

"Spooky" thinks Reggie, "I didn't think of my Mum and Dad; where did that come from?"

"You look a bit bored" says Basil to Jasmine, "come a bit closer, I've got something for you to play with here." Basil takes his belt off and hands it to Jasmine.

"See how shiny the buckle is, it's made of silver" says Basil as he puts his arm round Jasmine and pulls her to him. At that moment something clicks inside Reggie. He doesn't know why but this seems all wrong. A grown up doesn't put a young girl on his knee and then start taking off his clothes. Without thinking any further Reggie launches himself off the bookshelf onto the councillor's desk and starts to run up Basil's arm.

"Hells bells" mutters the startled Basil "there's a rat in my office!"

"Here we go again" thinks Reggie, as his thoughts turn towards Lord Carrington and his recent narrow escape at Barkley Hall. With one more lunge Reggie lands upon Basil's shoulder and reaching up, bites him as hard as he can on the ear.

"You dirty rat!" Shouts Basil in a passable imitation of James Cagney. "I'll have you for this!" Reggie jumps onto the side table where the councillor's secretary normally takes notation, but misses his footing (or should it be pawing) and falls to the floor.

"Ah ha!" Exclaims Basil "I've got you this time," and proceeds to try and stamp on Reggie. However without his belt, his trousers begin to fall around his ankles and as he takes aim; Basil falls over like a penguin in a skittle alley.

Jasmine's still holding Basil's belt when the door is flung open and Henrietta Lurch storms in.

"What is going on? She exclaims, "there's such a noise of banging and clattering". She then notices the councillor lying on the floor with his trousers around his ankles.

"Mr Bond I don't believe it" she utters in a rather 'Victor Meldrew' sort of way. There is a sadness in her voice as she secretly has a longing for Basil that's been hidden for years.

"I'm afraid Miss Lurch that there is a rat in here, would you please inform the janitor?" Says Basil trying to regain his composure as he hurriedly pulls up his trousers and tears the belt out of Jasmine's grasp before she can do anything.

"I don't think the rat is here any more" lies Jasmine as she'd seen Reggie hide under the desk, "I saw it disappear down a hole in the skirting board over there" she says, pointing to the far end of the room.

"Thanks Jasmine" thinks Reggie as he hides further under the desk.

"You're welcome" mouthes Jasmine silently and both she and Reggie think: "OMG!"

Jasmine realises that she actually didn't need to speak out loud for Reggie to 'hear' her so they carry on an amazing thought transference whilst she is travelling in her parent's car. The signals between them begin to fade as they move further away but they just have time to establish where they both live.

They realise that the distance between their respective abodes is less than a mile as Reggie resides in Hisbrand Walk by the sea and Jasmine is just the other side of the golf course backing onto the beach.

"You must come round and see my room" enthuses Jasmine, and Reggie just has time to reply before their 'thought' signals fade completely:

"As long as you've got some Twiglets I'll be there in spades!"

Chapter Seven

Donal's induction

Donal and Sam are sitting in the living room of their new abode, watching the sun go down and savouring a glass of wine together. Jasmine is upstairs in her room introducing Reggie to likely nooks and crannies to explore. She's sitting in the Lotus position in her favourite window seat using her tablet, whilst watching the furry rodent out of the corner of her eye, as he 'checks out the facilities'.

"How was your day?"Asks Samantha as she snuggles further into the sofa and closer to Donal.

"Unusual, and slightly surreal" replies Donal. "I met the big cheese for the second time, and he tried to rope me in to the annual Christmas do where most of the upper ranks do a turn. I guess he wants to show the men that the officers are as vulnerable as the next guy. Apparently it's good for morale and gives the men a chance to take the proverbial out of their superiors."

"Well as you're the new boy, I suppose it would be a quick way for the men at Division to get to know you?" Queries Sam, "you could do a few card tricks; you used to be really good at that, and you could employ Jazz as your assistant!"

"Oh yeh she'd love that!" Retorts Donal, "she'd run a mile rather than assist. She would be so embarrassed."

"I am a bit worried since we came back from the Town Hall" adds Sam, "she seems very quiet and not her normal carefree self and I sensed a strange atmosphere when we went back to pick her up between the secretary and Councillor Bond." Donal visually stiffens at the mention of Basil Bond's name.

"Should we ask her if anything happened whilst we were away?" Sam enquires.

"No, I'm sure she'll tell us if anything's wrong in her own time" counters Donal.

Jasmine is running down the stairs: "Did I hear my name taken in vain?" She ventures.

"Your Dad has a madcap idea to ask you to be his assistant conjuror at the forthcoming work do" says Sam winking at Donal in the hope that she can get away with turning the tables on the suggestion, and making it seem like his fault when Jasmine ridicules the idea.

Jasmine thinks for quite a while, turning her head wistfully back up towards her room, and eventually says: "I'll do it on one condition."

"Wow, name it!" Chorus her parents.

"You'll let us do a mind reading trick. I'll ask a member of the audience to take out an article and hold it in their hand whilst you are blindfolded and you'll tell them what it is."

"How will I know?" Asks Donal.

"We'll make up a code like so many hand squeezes for different items."

"How   will   you   know?"

"You'll just have to trust me. I'm like Mystic Meg!" Cries Jasmine.

"Talk about out of the frying pan into the fire!" Says Donal.

"Ain't that the truth" thinks Reggie as he had overheard the last few remarks and begins to realise the full implication of Jazz's statement.

~~~~~~~~~~~~~~~~~~~~~~~~~~~~~~~~

The day of the Christmas 'do' has come. There have been many rehearsals in the Jones's household to try and perfect the act. The Chief Constable David Doyle is on first and does a very good impression of 'Danny LaRue' the drag queen, which seems to go down well with the men for all the wrong reasons, but it appears to relax the room into not expecting too high a standard.

Next is Inspector Ross who has a fine Tenor voice and does a very passable rendition of 'Nessun Dorma'.

Now it is the turn of DS Jones and his glamorous assistant Jasmine, better known as 'Merlin and Lenora'. The act starts well with Donal ending three accomplished card tricks with the 'four aces' trick which draws a respected hush and then loud applause.

"Now Merlin will read your minds by knowing certain items that you are holding" begins Jasmine slightly nervously. "I shall place this blindfold, which has been verified by the Chief Constable as being completely legitimate, on Merlin. May we have a volunteer please?" A show of hands and Jasmine chooses the person closest to where Reggie is hiding under a seat.

"Please take any item from your pocket and show it to a few people around you but not high enough for me to see." The man reaches into his pocket and shows a comb. Jasmine squeezes Donal's hand twice which is their code for such an item.

"I think you're holding a comb" says Donal to applause.

"Ok can we have one more?" Says Jasmine. Detective Constable Rod Bull stands up and says:

"I've got an item." Rod is not a fan of Donal. He resents the fact that head office have sent down a new man and passed over his promotion to Detective Sergeant. He takes his watch off and before putting it in his hand, changes the time from three fifteen to ten pass four. Reggie's straining round the foot of the stairs to see this and just manages to spot the subterfuge before someone yells:

"Oy there's a rat in the room!"

"What only one!" Replies a wag on the other side of the hall, followed by much laughter. In the confusion Reggie manages to duck further under a cupboard but is now a long way from the action.

"You're holding a watch" says Donal to much applause and Rod holds it up but with the face towards him and away from the stage.

"Well Merlin let's see how good you really are" shouts Rod. "What time does my watch read?"

Silence. Jasmine squeezes four times.

"It's becoming clearer" mumbles Merlin, "it's four..." Jasmine's pumping his hand as fast as she can: "Ten."

"Fantastic" shouts Rod feeling a new respect and very puzzled by such a genuine piece of magic. The applause echoes round the hall and luckily for Reggie everyone seems to have forgotten about him. Merlin and Lenora take their bows amidst great applause but at this point the Chief Constable who has now changed back into his normal clothes stands up.

"This has been so good, could we have just one more go?" He pleads.

Jasmine looks worried. She knows Reggie's not in a strategic place but as Donal doesn't know how it works, he's feeling gung-ho about the situation.

"Yes Chief, fire away" he enthuses.

The Chief Constable stands, feels into his pocket and pulls out a clenched fist and holds both hands clenched in the air. Beads of sweat have broken out on Reggie's and Jasmine's faces. They know they don't know. Jasmine looks up at Donal with a face that only a daughter can give her Dad when she wants ultimate forgiveness and squeezes his hand once, meaning she just doesn't know.

"Well come on Merlin we're all waiting" says the Chief Constable encouragingly. Donal looks up, wipes away the bead of sweat emanating from his makeshift turban and says:

"I have...Absolutely nothing."

Complete silence. All eyes are on the Chief Constable. What's he going to say? What's he going to do?

He opens his hands and shows...Absolutely nothing.

The place erupts. Four burly coppers jump up on the stage and carry Donal shoulder high off into the wings. Sam and another Mum place Jasmine on their shoulders and carry her off too.

Reggie's lying on his back doing paw pumps in the air. What a day!

Chapter Eight

When Harry met the aliens

Every couple of weeks Harry likes to take his last glass of wine and retire to the boat deck to smoke a cigar. This is one of those occasions.

He had shared a lovely meal of Steak Diane with Clair and a surprisingly mellow bottle of 2010 Merlot. Clair could tell that Harry needed to enjoy that last glass, so suggested that he go and find a few Twiglets to give to Reggie, being sure that there were some on the boat, whilst she enjoyed her favourite TV programme.

Harry gazes up at the evening sky seeing each star and constellation appear as the sun sank lower. "What a great time of day; and night" he remarks to Reggie. He opens the fridge door situated in the cabin and notices some crab sticks. Reggie's favourite! This brings a chuckle to Harry because he knows what's coming. Reggie loves crab sticks even more than

Twiglets so Harry teases him with them whilst blowing a huge smoke ring with his cigar. Reggie knows that if he can jump through the ring, there will be a lovely reward of a crab stick, so launches into the air at the first sign of the ring. Harry always tries to catch Reggie, especially when the rings drifts towards the edge of the boat. It ends up with them both in a heap on the deck laughing like a couple of nine year olds. After which Harry resumes his seat with the glass of Merlot and cigar whilst Reggie curls up with a crab stick and Twiglet feast.

Harry is half way through his cigar when he notices lights shining at all angles coming from the sea. He peers into the semi darkness but the lights are still some way off the shore. He delves into the cabin to pick up his night binoculars and begins to scan the coast line. There is a small boat carrying a group of people looking very bedraggled and frightened. Harry guesses that this is no ordinary fishing vessel.

He had met D.S. Donal Jones at the police do where Donal and Jasmine performed their extraordinary act, and after chatting together the two families had exchanged numbers to get together in the future. They had talked about Harry building his boat and living on the coast. Harry remembers Donal's words to phone him at home if he sees anything untoward at sea, so he does just that.

"Keep an eye on the boat please Harry, but don't approach. I'll be there with the coastguard ASAP."

After fifteen minutes or so a car pulls up onto Harry's forecourt with lights extinguished. Donal and two other men alight and move towards the beach and Harry's boat.

"This is Jim and Pete from the coastguard" says Donal to Harry, "What is the situation?"

"The boat is still approximately fifty metres offshore and to the right of the rocks over there" says Harry pointing west along the coast.

"I'll call for a van and some extra officers to be on hand" ventures Pete. "It looks as if they'll come ashore very soon."

"You're probably right" counters Donal, "but just in case they try to go back out to sea, which would be highly dangerous, have we a boat nearby to call?"

"It could be another half an hour before it gets here" says Jim.

"You could use mine" interjects Harry, "it's ready to launch now and if I go out behind them it should stop them trying."

"Harry that's very generous; Jim could go with you" says Donal, "meanwhile we'll wait here until the boat grounds and Pete can take the car and drive west along Hisbrand Walk so we won't miss anyone."

Just as they finish talking a huge coach arrived looking very much like 'Kit', the car in Knight Rider only ten times bigger.

"This must be the new bus that we've been hearing about" whispers Jim in reverent tones. "It's meant to be a very hush-hush collaboration with the government and the space agency to try and keep up with the overwhelming overload of immigration.

We've heard some detail about how space age it is and if it's a tenth of that, we're in for a real treat."

As he is speaking the bus pulls onto the stones at the edge of the beach and centres itself on an area where the boat appears to be landing. Two arms come out from either end and push into the stones, and a massive canopy on hydraulic ramps, extends out towards the beach. When all movement has finished, huge lights come on as if the sun has been turned on but with it's own umbrella, as the light is not blinding, but gives a serene glow to a fifty metre area around, and in front of the migrants.

"OMG" says Harry "it's like 'Close Encounters Of The Third Kind' but somehow we seem to be the aliens!"

He remembers the film of that name and fully expects a music synthesiser to blast out the five notes: D E C drop an octave C G, but that doesn't happen. Instead a team of medics in white coats and nurses come from the bus and approach the migrants as they disembark.

There are approximately twenty people including one woman carrying a baby and another lady who needs help to walk. There are three teenage children who look very distraught and four older men who seem to be organising the rest.

As this is unfolding Harry and Jim launch the boat and make a sweep of the surrounding area, but as no-one seems to be trying to get away from the craft, they return to shore. Many of the migrants are being taken to the bus by the people in white coats and some are helped by the nurses whilst a machine that resembles a moon buggy is approaching the lady who can not walk. She is helped to stand as the buggy comes nearer and a board like a stretcher top extends from the machine and holds her in place. The contraption then gently lowers the woman onto the top of the buggy and proceeds back to the bus. As it traverses the uneven terrain of the beach the huge wheels of the buggy move up and down whilst keeping the main frame completely flat.

"I keep looking round expecting to see John Williams and his orchestra playing the themes from ET and Star Wars at any moment!" Says Donal to Harry who has just rejoined him.

"This is surreal, it's like something out of a futuristic movie" agrees Harry.

Just then Clair arrives. She has picked up Reggie and given him a cuddle and another crab stick so he is very happy.

"I was coming out to see if I could make drinks for anyone but the situation seems to be well in hand" she says viewing the scene with admiration and a certain amount of awe.

"Apparently the government have plans to build fifty of these buses but it's still very secret" whispers Jim in a conspiratorial voice.

"I shouldn't worry about us telling anyone" replies Harry, "they'd never believe us anyway!"

Chapter Nine

Reggie goes east

Chief Constable David Doyle is having a meeting with Donal at his house and they are discussing Councillor Bond and his association with Alan Trask who is Bond's brother-in-law. They only know that Trask is linked to a company in Lithuania which has massive Euro funding. Every time they have a lead as to the source of the illegal contraband there is a leak and nothing comes of the information. The only knowledge they have is that the company and fund have been helped to be set up and approved by the MEP Sir Charles Grimwall but there, the trail ends.

Reggie is sharing a chilled out evening with Jasmine and he overhears Donal's discussion with the Chief and that the only way they can catch the illegal importers is if they learn the identity of the source of their nefarious activities in Hong Kong, but every time they have a lead there is a leak in this country.

Reggie thinks through this latest development with Jasmine and decides to visit his cousin Ronda in Hong Kong.

Shortly after making this plan Harry and Clair are visiting Sovereign Harbour to watch the debut performance of Eric Clapton's new documentary called 'Life in twelve bars' so Reggie cadges a lift and steals aboard a pilot boat to Southampton docks where he manages to hide away in a slow boat to China and sits back and waits...And waits...

"Thank heaven for planes" he thinks to himself as the fourth day passes and he's still on the steamer heading East.

There are many of his fellow species on board and to say that his time is dull would be an understatement. He meets a colourful character named Salty Sam who is in charge of the Galley so he's able to get tit bits most evenings when the crew have finished their meal. One evening Salty Sam offers him a plate of ratatouille and apart from the name of the dish, Reggie really didn't fancy it and his look towards Salty must have shown his distaste.

"How can anyone eat something with 'rat' in the title when it has no meat in it?" He thinks to himself, not wishing to be churlish to Sam or imply that he has any cannibalistic tendencies.

Sam notices Reggie's reluctance to partake in the ratatouille experience and gives him some biscuits.

Apart from all these goings on, it had given him time to reflect on his cousin in downtown Hong Kong who is a rather colourful character. By day she is a Feng shui expert and helps the local rat population situate their 'abodes' in the best way.

"It's no good having a south facing entrance to your burrow" she'd say, "because the sun will shine straight into the hole making it easier for predators to see you before you have even reached the entrance. Always have a north facing burrow."

By night however Ronda dances in the local ratatorium in a distinctly risqué routine under the stage name of 'Lucy Lastic'. "Think Jessica Rabbit and you're getting close," muses Reggie.

When Reggie finally arrives in Kowloon he is met by Ronda who says he can stay with her family, and after a quick debriefing of Reggie's predicament, offers the following advice:

"You need to meet a cousin of mine who often frequents the local administration offices. His name is Wang and he'll get you to the export office where you can hopefully discover information about your man. Wang will stay with you unless you speak fluent Cantonese!"

The next day Reggie and Wang are situated in the office on top of a shelf filled with dusty ledgers. Wang has brought some rice cakes and water because he knows this could be a lengthy wait.

On the second day they strike a lucky break as Wang recognises that one of the officials is talking about 'Trask Enterprises' and that there is a shipment due to leave in three days time. The representative from Trask is coming to the office to finalise the details. Reggie and Wang agree to meet back on that day.

The day arrives and they have just taken up their strategic positions when the representative from Trask enters and bows to the official in charge. They exchange greetings and the Trask rep gives a package to the clerk. After pocketing the package in his jacket the clerk begins the discussion. 'T42 ELC1D' is the registration number of the lorry that will be transporting the real merchandise when it arrives at Dover. There are two other lorries acting as decoys holding just enough low level contraband to illicit a fine and confiscation of the goods, but no prosecutions.

"I've got to remember this number" thinks Reggie and he can recall Percy Potts saying that if you needed to remember a list, or random letters and numbers, try to tie each bit to something that is already familiar.

"T forty two, T forty two" repeats Reggie, "T four two, T four two and two for tea! Got it." He could remember the old song that he had often heard Percy singing.

"Now onto E L C one D; El is a Spanish preposition as in 'El Toro'; the bull and 'C one D' could be CiD which is Donal's job so; Spanish detective! So the whole thing is Tea for two and Spanish detective. Got it!"

Percy would be proud of him. He had often heard Pam and Percy doing the crossword together. Somehow they needed each other to complete the whole thing and it seemed much more fun!

However there is a big problem because Reggie realises that if his only way home is by boat it will take him longer to get back than the shipments. He realises he'll have to get on a jet but how?

Chapter Ten

Reggie goes west

That evening Reggie visits Ronda at the ratatorium which is situated next door to ChunkKing Mansions where she is doing her 'Lucy Lastic' dance.

"What a hoot" he thinks to himself.

The place is abuzz with excitement. Rodents dancing everywhere. Red Whiskered Bulbuls looking like waiters, flapping their white tipped wings and making their 'kick-a-roo' cry which sounds very like: "Nice to meet you".

Mice eating all the cheese and knocking over honey pots that have been filled with water. Mayhem everywhere, but huge fun!

After the dance has finished Reggie goes backstage to Ronda's dressing room and, after congratulating her on the performance, tells her about his 'time' predicament. Ronda thinks for a long while until

Reggie thinks she may have fallen asleep, but suddenly exclaims:

"Got it! The house next door to where I normally reside is occupied by Waylee who's in the diplomatic corp and she often travels to the UK as a courier with the Embassy. I'm sure we can hide you in one of the diplomatic bags on her next trip which with any luck will be in the next few days".

After two days kicking his heels (paws) Reggie is secreted aboard flight LGW101 on an A380 jet. As he gets closer to England he begins to 'feel' or 'hear' bits of messages which make him think of Jasmine. Spookily Jazz is picking up a 'vibe' about Reggie around the same time and is quite excited as she knows what he's been trying to do, and is pleased that it feels like he must be on the way back. She keeps picking up London Gatwick in her thoughts and comes to the conclusion that somehow Reggie is making his way there.

That morning Jasmine convinces her Dad that she really has a definite interest in aeroplanes and the only one left that she hasn't seen is the new A380 airbus which luckily is arriving at Gatwick from Hong Kong in two hours time. Donal knows when he sees that pleading look in his daughter's eyes that he might as well give in gracefully and, as it's his day off, does exactly that. He's secretly pleased as he has just bought a new Tesla electric car and is keen for an excuse to try it out.

Jazz has taken her rucksack filled with binoculars (to spot all the planes that she's really interested in) and some cheese and Reggie's favourite: Twiglets! When they arrive at the airport Donal drops Jazz off at the main entrance while he parks the car and Jazz makes her way to the arrivals terminal. She takes a seat in the busy lounge area and luckily the A380 airbus is parked very close to the window so she is able to take a few pics on her phone to keep up the 'authenticity' of her new found hobby. She finds herself being very impressed by the plane as it's head and shoulders so much bigger than all the other planes and a really impressive shape and style.

"Maybe it's not such a white lie after all" she muses. Just then she hears a rustle near her back where the rucksack is seated and the side flap is moving. Then she can hear some crunching sounds and it looks like her rucksack is a jumping bean!

"Reggie! It's fantastic that you're back but don't jump around too much otherwise you'll have airport security on us" Jazz thinks.

"It's great to be back" rethinks Reggie "and thanks for the snack."

After a while Donal appears and asks Jazz how she's been getting on with her plane spotting.

"Oh it's superb" she says pointing at the airbus and showing her dad the pics. "Thank you so much Dad for bringing me." Jazz gives her dad a big hug and although a little surprised by his daughter's public affection, Donal feels a warm glow and is pleased that he gave in so gracefully.

They decide to have brunch at the airport before setting off for home. All the time they have been eating, Jazz and Reggie have been able to 'talk' through most of the detail surrounding Reggie's trip and have formulated a plan as to how to be able to tell Donal without arousing suspicion that Jazz's 'evidence' has come from a rat! On the drive home Jasmine opens up to Donal:

"Dad, I know I haven't spoken about what happened at the town hall until now because it upset me a lot and I couldn't deal with my feelings and explain at the same time. Councillor Bond tried to get me to sit on his knee and if it hadn't been for the intervention of a rat running up Bond's arm, I don't know what would have happened. Unfortunately Bond's secretary Miss Lurch came into the room at this point and although she could see Bond was in a compromised position, I don't think she would corroborate my version of events."

Jazz realises she is sounding almost like her dad and she obviously listens to his legalise talk more than she thought! Donal is alarmed by his daughter's revelation but so pleased that she is able to talk to him about it. Jazz continues:

"The reason I'm mentioning this is because when I was sitting in the boardroom" (and this is where the duplicity starts) "before they came in to where I was sitting, I overheard Bond and Miss Lurch talking about shipments coming in to the country, and one in particular that seemed very important to Bond. He kept on talking about the importance of this particular lorry. He mentioned it so often that I jotted down the number of the lorry and the day it was due to arrive in the UK. He also mentioned a person who was their main contact in Hong Kong and that under no circumstance was anyone else to take a call from this person and if he did call, he was to be put through to Bond no matter what he was doing."

"Do you remember the name of this person?" Asks Donal.

"I think it was Alan Tusk or Alan Tryst something like that" replies Jazz, hoping that her attempt at remembering is making the subterfuge that this is a long ago memory more believable.

"Could it have been Alan Trask?" Asks Donal.

"Yes! That was it!" She says enthusiastically.

Donal's mind is in a whirl with so many mixed emotions. He hates the fact that Jazz has been touched by Bond and wants to punch his lights out, but getting taken off the force and prosecuted for hitting an overweight older man doesn't seem the best course of action. Especially as his superiors at the Met expect him to find the main source of the high level leaks in the area.

"Jazz, I'm so proud of you for the way that you've handled this incident with Bond and be rest assured he will pay for his indiscretions. Thank you so much for the other information as I'm sure the 'powers that be' will be very interested in what you've told me."

Chapter Eleven

The detective

The magical sea mists float serenely across the dwellings in Pevensey Bay giving an ethereal appearance of them flying. This is the view that Reggie has from his vantage point on the wall by the bus stop near Cooden Sea Road. Reggie is waiting here so that he can leap off the wall onto Jazz's rucksack as she disembarks from the bus. He can only do this if she is on her own though. Last week he had frightened the life out of Mrs Perrin who saw him do this and she let out a scream.

Soon they are ensconced in Jasmine's room at the house in Maple Road. Jazz has spent some time on her homework whilst Reggie explored the Twiglet box. Her homework now finished Jazz has taken up her favourite position on her window seat and Reggie is curled up on her shoulder nuzzled into her neck. This is his cosy spot especially when it is cold outside.

Today the intrepid pair discuss (by thoughts) the capture of Ollie, and are hatching a plan to try and rescue him from the clutches of Ledmen his abductor. Reggie has found out through Ollie's family that he is being held at Ledmen's cottage which is on the Bexingham Estate. They can reach the cottage by walking through the woods at the back of Maple Walk. After a half an hour trudge through the undergrowth Jazz, with Reggie hitching a ride in her rucksack, comes to a clearing and a large field containing many mobile homes. Although it is early evening, it is still quite light and warm. The pathway weaves past the mobile structures at a slight distance and as they pass the third one Jazz notices a lady sitting in front of the fourth. She has a gaily coloured headscarf round her head and a lovely flowing gown that trails around her bare feet.

"Hello Jasmine, I've been expecting you" she says, "my name is Rose Almond."

Jazz is taken aback by this revelation but quickly regains her composure and replies: "Hello Ms Almond, it's lovely to meet you, but I'm surprised that you know me."

"Ah well, the mystic wonders of the world are not always clear to the uninitiated" Rose replies; she was being a tad naughty with the truth here because she had met Jasmine's mother Samantha a few times on Hastings Pier, where she worked occasionally, and Sam had often mentioned her daughter by name. She had then seen Sam and Jazz together in the town.

"And please call me Rose, because even though we haven't met before, I'm sure I can help you with your quest."

"I can't believe she can see into the future" muses Reggie, "most clairvoyants are charlatans but just very good at body language I've been told."

"Yes but not all of us" replies Rose with a knowing smile on her face. Reggie immediately turns a crimson brown and hops from one paw to another feeling most uncomfortable.

"You can 'hear' Reggie as well?" Retorts Jazz to Rose.

"Yes, and you are very gifted to have this ability" ventures Rose. "Anyway tell me about your reason for being here."

Jazz outlines the story of Ledmen and his taking of Ollie and that they are here to try and retrieve the owl before he becomes too reliant on his keeper, and won't be able to leave.

"There is a problem with the alarm system that Ledmen has set up" says Rose, "any flight movements of the birds will set it off."

Just then Aloysius turns up and silently perches next to Reggie: "Sorry I'm late guys, how are things going?"

Reggie outlines the problem to the owl and he nods as only owls can, at each point, moving his head through a hundred and eighty degrees.

"Leave it to me" Aloysius says to Reggie after a lengthy pause, "I think I have a solution." Reggie conveys this information to Rose and Jazz because they don't speak Owl and the mood in the camp is lightened.

"Owls are very wise" concludes Rose, "I look forward to the outcome."

Aloysius has asked the intrepid band to hide in the woods just out of sight of Ledmen's abode with a pair of wire cutters. As they settle down as comfortably as possible with a small view of the cottage, a very faint swoosh is heard as Aloysius lands on the roof of the outdoor accommodation containing the birds. He holds onto the top beam of the structure and flaps his wings violently, making no sound but generating a huge vortex of air that sets off the alarm. As this happens the owl flies to a nearby branch just out of sight. Searchlights come on, movement and confusion abound with much scurrying around and Ledmen appears looking very dishevelled. He trains the searchlights onto the surrounding area and checks that the birds are still in their abode whilst trying not to disturb them. He knows that any change to their routine can make them fractious the next day and in turn diminish their performance. After a complete walk round of the cottage and a thorough search of the grounds, Ledmen finally retires and calm is restored.

Cue Aloysius! The second and third time that this happens Rose and Jazz are beginning to feel sorry for Ledmen, but not too much! After the fourth time Ledmen decides to turn off the alarm as he's convinced there must be a fault in the system. He stumbles back to the cottage and slams the door in frustration.

Rose and Jazz decide to wait half an hour before attempting phase two of the operation to be on the safe side. Aloysius makes a precautionary pass of the cottage but can see no sign of life and gives the all clear. Jazz steals forward with the wire cutters that she borrowed from her Dad's tool box and manages to find Ollie and three other birds who have recently been 'acquired'. Jazz cuts free the feathered four but leaves the others as they have been with Ledmen for so long, they would struggle to return to a wild state, so are happy to stay.

"Reggie and company" says Ollie, "you've excelled yourselves and returned the favour in spades. Thank you so much."

Rose learns through the grapevine that Ledmen has since made no complaint about the incident.

It's as if it never happened.

Chapter Twelve

Reggie gets into hot water

Pamela Potts is sitting in the window seat of her apartment trying to finish the crossword.

"A shelter from the rain, nine letters" she reads under her breath and notices that two other words that she's already worked out give 'b' as the third letter and 'g' as the eighth.

"I wish Percy were here" she muses, thinking of her cousin Percival Potts, "he's a wizard at these more obscure words." Just then there's a knock at the door and before she can move or shout out to come in, the door opens to reveal her cousin Percy.

"Just finished the round Pam and thought it would be nice to catch up with you; and you also make the best cup of tea in town!"

"Percy I was just thinking of you," replies Pam and tells him the crossword clue and what letters she has from other clues.

"Ombrifuge" says Percy, "a shelter from the rain."

"You're so clever" retorts Pam, "is there anything you don't know?"

"Yeh, when's the tea arriving?"

Pam works at the council offices as a coordinator and over tea she discusses with Percy the rather irregular goings on between Councillor Bond and some of his other associates, in particular Alan Trask, but comes to the conclusion that they don't have enough information to take the matter any further.

"Let's talk about something more pleasant" says Percy, "when are you moving to your new house in Maple Walk?"

"In a fortnight" replies Pam, "I can't wait, I'm so looking forward to it."

Reggie usually spends his Saturday afternoons watching Harry work on his boat and enjoying the odd tasty tit-bit which Harry will throw his way. Harry also has a penchant for a Twiglet and he really enjoys watching Reggie catch them in his mouth like a well trained dog. Reggie loves it too because the more he catches, the more Harry throws! However today Harry and Clair have gone to Sovereign Harbour for the day so Reggie decides to visit his second home, namely Jasmine's place in Maple Walk. When Reggie arrives he usually surprises Jazz by shinning up the tree by the side of her window and, after making sure no-one is in with her, taps on the window and waves his paws wildly in the air. This usually makes Jazz laugh out loud but today she gingerly comes to the window to let Reggie in looking very much the worse for wear.

"This is not a good day Reggie. I'm always glad to see you but I have a really high temperature and generally not feeling well. I'd hate you to catch anything off me so I've left you some goodies downstairs."

"Oh Jazz I hope you're better soon" replies Reggie as he scuttles off down the stairs. As he's enjoying a snack by the kitchen door he can hear Donal and

Samantha talking in the snug next door so he decides to have a listen. They're talking in hushed whispers which makes it far more intriguing. Donal is saying:

"Is Jazz in bed? Because I would rather she doesn't hear us talking about Bond. It could be traumatic for her."

"Yes she went to bed half an hour ago and really is quite poorly so I don't think she'll be getting up," replies Sam. "What's the problem with the councillor?"

"Well you know I told you how Jazz opened up to me on the way back from Gatwick? I have evidence against Bond but there is a greater threat from inside the force down here and that person is linked to Bond. I just can't get the proof against this person that I need and until I do, Head Office don't want me to bring Bond to account as this will close the whole operation down and the main source in Whitehall will still be a mystery. One of the detective's is interviewing Bond tomorrow at his house in Clavering but this is just a formality to allay suspicion. Everyone at the council offices involved with importing would be routinely interviewed in light of what has happened."

Reggie is devastated to hear this. Poor Jazz! After all she went through with that dastardly devil Bond. Reggie decides to pay a visit to Councillor Bond's abode. He knows Clavering Walk very well as the road backs on to Cooden golf course.

Bond is sitting in his Jacuzzi which is situated on the rear deck of the house overlooking the golf course. As Reggie approaches the area he sees that there is another person in the hot tub with Bond namely Detective Constable Rodney Bull. Reggie scrambles along a tree branch overlooking Bond and his guest. At that moment the jacuzzi springs into life and the water bubbles and gurgles noisily. This is a bonus for Reggie, as both men have to speak loudly to hear each other. They talk of the Lithuanian section of their operation bringing counterfeiting equipment and many fake passports by boat to Normans Bay in three day's time. Rod will oversee the delivery and take it to Sir Charles Grimwall's house situated in Hisbrand Walk where the fake identities will be produced.

This is definitely the break that will confirm the name of the mole which head office have been after, but how can Reggie get this information to them? Jazz is sick, and even if they 'thought' communicate, how can she convincingly pass on the information from an unknown source? Whilst this is spinning around in Reggie's mind he fails to spot a red kite zooming in on him. He suddenly feels this huge rush of air as the red kite's wing knocks into him. Unfortunately for the bird, instead of knocking Reggie out, it knocks him into the hot-tub!

Councillor Bond looks startled by the splash next to him: "What the heck was that?" he exclaims.

Rod shrugs his shoulders and declares: "Wow there's a massive bird hovering in the tree above, maybe it dislodged a branch."

Reggie plummets to the bottom of the hot-tub and spots a bulbous toe waggling excitedly. He decides to give it a tickle and then attempt to vacate the jacuzzi as quickly as possible as it's a bit too hot in the water. Bond feels this tickling sensation on his foot and his mind goes into overdrive.

"Maybe a lizard fell out of the tree and is eyeing up my foot as a meal" he ponders. With this thought racing through his mind Bond leaves the jacuzzi as if he were at the tautest end of a bungee jump, almost imitating Tom the cat from the old cartoon 'Tom and Jerry'. Rod is made of sterner stuff so plunges his head under the water to try and see what form this interloper takes. Reggie has surfaced by this time and taking his chance, leap frogs from Rod's back onto the opposite side of the hot-tub to Bond. As the two conspirators are trying to regain their composure, Reggie hot foots it to Ollie's domain to calm down after another near miss. What a day!

Ollie listens to Reggie's predicament about getting the information to Donal without arousing a major amount of scepticism. After a short while, which seems endless to Reggie, Ollie says:

"Why don't you visit Rose who can read your thoughts? She can pass on the information to Samantha and it will be up to Sam to try and persuade Donal that it might be worth following up."

"Ollie you're a genius" enthuses Reggie, "I knew there was a reason we had to save you!"

"Cheeky rat" retorts Ollie and he makes a swipe at Reggie's ear, but misses, and they both fall on the ground laughing.

Chapter Thirteen

Intrigue

Jasmine's cold hadn't developed into a full blown one so she and Reggie are perched on the end of her bed with the door open trying to listen to the conversation downstairs. Samantha is talking:

"I've only known Rose Almond since we've been here, but everything she's foretold about our situation and you being in the police would have been hard to get one hundred percent right, as she didn't know me before and has still never met you. It seems a long shot but she was so specific about the time and place of this boat coming in to Normans Bay that I think you should give it some serious consideration."

"The problem is" begins Donal, "that we're too short of men to cover every tip off, even from our well known informers. As you're so adamant, I don't mind covering it and I'll ask Harry to come along to observe in case there's more than one person. I'll inform Customs and ask them to keep a phone line available in case we need back up."

The drop is expected at two thirty in the morning. Donal and Harry set off to a high point which overlooks most of the beach at Normans Bay. The moonlight is leaving an eerie glow over the whole bay and as the time approaches two thirty they see a car approaching from the Pevensey direction. Donal has his infra-red night binoculars so watches as the car halts, puts out its lights and a figure emerges.

"Good God!" Exclaims Donal, "it's Rod Bull. What the heck is he doing here? No-one else at the station knows about this."

There is a low throbbing sound emanating from the sea as a powerful engined boat with no lights on approaches the shore. Three men are observed by the onshore spectators as the engines are cut and silence reigns. Two of the men are Lithuanians Thomas and Kurt who have offered Rod Bull a consignment he cannot refuse. They know that the only way to muscle in on the UK market is to bring very enticing booty and this is exactly what   their cargo does.

The counterfeiting equipment is of the highest quality and very expensive so you can imagine they are very cautious. Rod Bull signals a code from his laser light to the men on the boat and they anchor off shore. Thomas and Kurt get out of the boat into a small dinghy and come to the beach. They pass a package and a briefcase to Bull, who immediately gives a different package back to Thomas and the two of them head off along Hisbrand Walk whilst Kurt sets off in the opposite direction towards the Beachlands Estate in Normans Bay. As they all fade into the night the boat's engine springs into life and is driven away at some speed. Donal manages to take the number of the boat and calls customs who alert the coastguard and agree to send two officers to Hisbrand Walk without delay. Harry follows the single man called Kurt with strict instructions from Donal not to approach him; just observe. Donal follows Bull and the other man at a safe distance along Hisbrand Walk where they eventually enter a rather fine looking house with many lights on. Donal stops a safe distance from the house after noting its name and number. He calls Harry and asks who lives at 'Portabello' number sixteen and receives a shocked response:

"That's Sir Charles Grimwall's place, wow I don't envy you tackling him. He's a crusty old so-and-so at the best of times" says Harry.

"How are things with you?" Enquires Donal.

"Just following the mark into Marine Avenue on the Beachlands Estate," replies Harry feeling very James Bond about the situation.

At that moment a car approaches from the station end of Hisbrand Walk and Donal flags it down with his torch. Two men alight from the vehicle and on approaching Donal, greet him and introduce themselves. They turn out to be the two customs officers Tom Wait and Jerry Sanders.

"Yes we've heard all the cat and mouse jokes before" sighs Tom, "what's the situation?"

Donal realises that time is of the essence so, without preamble, quickly fills them in regarding the situation. The three men leave the car parked on the side and walk to the front door. Donal tugs on a huge bell pull at the side of the oak door and more lights come on. Eventually after a long delay the door is opened and a man dressed in a tuxedo, presumably the butler, enquires as to what they want especially at this time of night.

"We'd like to speak with Sir Charles and Detective Bull who we know has just entered the premises" begins Donal, showing his warrant card as he is speaking.

"Come into the drawing room gentlemen" replies the butler, "I'll let Sir Charles know that you're here." After another lengthy wait Sir Charles Grimwall appears looking rather discombobulated and slightly out of breath.

"What can I do for you gentlemen?" He begins "I'm surprised to see you as well as Detective Bull, as I assumed we had the situation in hand."

"What is the situation sir?" Enquires Donal.

"Well the suspect has been arrested by Detective Bull and the fake documents have been retrieved" furthers Sir Charles.

Donal is completely taken aback by this revelation and can only assume that both Sir Charles and Bull are very bad poker players, as this has to be the biggest bluff in the history of Texas Hold'em. At this juncture Bull enters the room with a very furtive looking Thomas.

"Evening Detective Sergeant Jones" starts Bull, "yes I've arrested this man who I have been working undercover to apprehend."

At this point Tom Wait turns to the furtive man who he thought didn't seem to understand what was going on. Tom tried two or three different dialects until he got a flicker of recognition from Thomas and began to speak in Lithuanian to him. Roughly translated he told the man what Detective Bull and Sir Charles were proposing.

"You filthy svine" Thomas says to Bull and pulls a gun from his pocket.

"Don't be stupid" shouts Donal but Bull has already started to grapple with the Lithuanian. Suddenly there is a shot and a gurgling noise is heard as Thomas falls to the floor with blood flowing from the clothing round his stomach.

Bull is left holding the gun as the Lithuanian's hand falls from the trigger.

"That seems to be a lucky break Detective Bull" said Jerry Sanders, "especially as the man dying on the floor is the only witness who can refute your story." As Jerry is speaking he is trying to stem the flow of blood but with little success.

"Quickly fetch a sheet that we can use as a tourniquet" says Jerry, even though he knows it to be a futile gesture. The man is dying and Jerry knows that you cannot put a tourniquet round his stomach. After calling for an ambulance and sitting everyone down as calmly as the situation allows, Donal says:

"We're going to need to make a thorough search of your premises Sir Charles."

"I'm afraid unless you have a search warrant that will not be possible" replies the knight.

"You're forgetting that as Her Majesty's customs officers we are allowed to search any dwelling that we feel has hidden contraband and this certainly fits the bill" interjects Tom. "So if you would all stay in here, Officer Sanders and I will make a start."

"Is there anything that you would like to add to your story?" Donal asks Bull, making sure that he has taken the gun and secured it in an evidence bag.

"You're making a big mistake which will come out when the Chief Constable hears of this" pontificates Sir Charles. Meanwhile Bull remains quiet and pensive and does not answer Donal's question.

After much banging and crashing the two customs officers come back into the drawing room accompanied by the butler. They had kept him with them at all times so that they had an independent witness. Tom places a bag on the floor and asks Sir Charles:

"Have you any explanation for this suitcase full of counterfeiting equipment that we found behind a false wall in your bedroom?"

"I shall make no further comments without a solicitor present" says Sir Charles, "except to add this is a gross invasion of my privacy."

At this point Detective Bull moves closer to Donal and says in a hushed tone: "I need to speak with Commander Atkins before I make any further comments."

"Ok" replies Donal, "but before that I would ask Sir Charles to accompany me to the station so that we may explore this situation further. And as this is now a crime scene, Tom could you stay here until I send a police officer to take over from you?"

Sir Charles Grimwall begins to argue but realises that this is futile as the police will not let him stay under the circumstances, and Tom nods in agreement.

Donal is in a difficult situation because he would also like to restrain Detective Rodney Bull but realises that until he speaks to the Commander, who is second only in seniority to the Chief Constable, he is treading on dangerous political ground. All Donal can add as a caution to Bull is that he should return to the station and have no contact with Grimwall.

Chapter Fourteen

Follow that man

Harry is still waiting in Marine Avenue and is pretty sure that the third suspect has gone into one of three dwellings. It is difficult to be more precise as it is so dark and at this late hour there are no street lights on in the road so Harry texts Donal with this information. Donal has just ensconced Sir Charles Grimwall in the back of the police car so phones Harry back, before he gets in to accompany Grimwall to the station.

"Harry thank you so much for your help and I apologise for keeping you hanging on for so long. I'll explain when we next get together but there has been a fatality here so please make an exit as soon as possible and I'll put customs onto it first thing in the morning."

"Okay Donal, wow it's never a dull moment in your job is it? replies Harry, trying to sound flippant, but was secretly relieved that he can now wend his way home.

Unbeknown to Harry whilst all this has been going on Reggie had crept into Harry's hood of his big jacket. Harry rarely uses the hood as he has many hats that he likes to wear. Tonight he is wearing his Fedora. Reggie had fallen asleep whilst Harry was walking. The gentle side to side movement and the fleecy lining of the hood had all contributed to his somnolent state, but he now awoke to overhear the phone conversation between Harry and Donal, so decides that his best bet is to creep out of Harry's jacket and to see if he can find the correct house. As he scurries off towards the first of the houses he looks back to see Harry take a torch from his pocket and walk briskly down the lane, shining towards the potholes to avoid.

One of the lights is on in the first house so Reggie finds a cat flap at the back of the property and goes in. The house is occupied by a little old lady who, with the most vivid imagination in the world, doesn't look much like a smuggler. House number two is more like a run down mobile home. There are broken blinds hanging at jaunty angles in the windows and a fairly large chunk of wood missing from the front door. All good news to Reggie as he is able to walk straight in through the hole in the door. He makes his way to the kitchen and sees a thin wiry looking man making a hot drink which he is stirring as if his life depends on it. Some of the liquid sprays out of the mug as the man stirs but he doesn't take any notice.

"Seems a very sloppy sort of individual" thinks Reggie. "Typical gangster to me!"

The wiry man takes a swig from the mug and almost spits it out. He turns to a cupboard and adds two more spoonfuls of sugar to the concoction and begins his swirling motions again. He tastes again and giving a sigh of satisfaction moves to the next room which has a bed in one corner and some heavy curtains at the window. Reggie decides that as he hasn't seen any lights or movement from the last dwelling when he was outside, this must be the right venue. He notices some cheese left in the kitchen so takes a small piece and scrambles onto a wide beam above the kitchen door. He is just settling down on his beam for the rest of the night to finish his lump of cheese when there is the sound of footsteps approaching. The door is cautiously opened and a hooded figure steps into the room. The wiry man hears the sounds and enters the kitchen from the bedroom. The two men greet each other and the hooded man calls wiry man Kurt. They begin talking in a foreign language and after a short conversation Kurt hands hooded man a package which he opens and takes out a wad of notes and hands them to Kurt. Meanwhile Kurt has been making two hot drinks on the kitchen worktop. As he takes the drinks to the two easy chairs at the other end of the kitchen, the hooded man takes a knife from the magnetic rack and in one swift movement lunges at Kurt landing the knife through the back of his neck. He pulls the knife out as Kurt sinks to the floor and wipes off the blade and returns it to the rack. He walks to the front door, turns around to take one final look at his dastardly deed; and this causes Reggie's undoing.

He is so shocked by the speed at which a seemingly innocent meeting could turn so quickly into a horror movie that he loses his footing and falls off the beam above hooded man's head! As he falls his front paw scrapes against hooded man's face, drawing blood, and as he tries to save himself, he bites onto part of the hood. This rips off so Reggie finds himself spreadeagled at the feet of Detective Bull!

"Arghh you slimy little rat, I'll tear you apart!" Exclaims Bull.

"Not so much of the little; and it's Mr Rat to you" thinks Reggie as he makes a dash for an opening below the sink.

Fortunately as the mobile home is in a poor state of repair there are many gaps in the kitchen units and Reggie can keep well out of Bull's way. After a while of stomping around trying to unearth the rodent Bull checks that he has cleaned the knife properly, that there are are no tell tale signs of his presence, and leaves.

"OMG" thinks Reggie, "thank goodness Harry had left otherwise he might have been confronted by Bull as well."

After what seems an age, and when Reggie can no longer hear footsteps, he gingerly pokes his whiskers around the cupboard door. Kurt is lying on his side as Reggie tiptoes past, but just as he draws level with his shoulders, Kurt makes a final gasp and his whole body turns towards Reggie and his arm and hand pin the rodent to the floor. There is no other movement, so Reggie assumes that this was an involuntary act from a dying man, so all he has to do is get out from underneath this very heavy dead weight. As he tries to wriggle free Reggie suddenly realises that in all the commotion, he is still biting onto Bull's hood remnant, so using his two front paws he disentangles the cloth from his tooth and squeezes out from under Kurt's outstretched hand.

"I've had some hairy days in my life" he thinks, "but this one beats the lot!"

Chapter Fifteen

The dénouement

Detective Sergeant Donal Jones has asked Henrietta Lurch to come to the station to help the police with their enquiries. Henrietta has always maintained Councillor Bond's innocence regarding the incident with him and Jasmine Jones. However Donal is now presenting her with all the information that he has on Bond's nefarious activities with illegally importing contraband items.

"Miss Lurch," begins Donal "I applaud your loyalty to your work colleagues, but there comes a time when the actions of certain individuals, takes them over a line of no return. I feel that that is what has happened, and is happening now, at the council offices. Councillor Bond has put you in charge of much of the paperwork involved with his overseas activities except for one section from Lithuania.

This file and the individual Alan Trask are involved in this section of Bond's goings on."

Donal notices Henrietta physically stiffen as the name Trask is mentioned. Henrietta knows that he is the husband of Bond's sister Deirdre.

"The point is Sergeant that by your own admission, I don't deal with this side of Councillor Bond's activities so why should I know anything untoward about them?"

"I'm sure that you know Alan Trask and his wife Deirdre, and I know that you socialise with them on occasion with Bond."

"This is true but it doesn't mean that we talk about work at these gatherings."

"Maybe not" furthers Donal, "but there are certain aspects that I feel I should make you aware of."

Henrietta has been expecting this and steals herself for the expected list of contraband items.

She is not a bad woman but by the time she realised how many things she was involved in, it was too late to go back without resigning and this job was all she had.

Donal itemises the list in front of Henrietta and it takes many minutes to read through them, but Henrietta manages to keep poker faced throughout, mainly because she had handled the details, so expects what he initially tells her.

"There is one area which you may not be aware of" adds Donal, "and that is relating to a lorry that was intercepted two days ago. We have proof that this was a shipment specifically originated by Trask, who is Bond's CEO of his overseas company. The lorry was hiding many of the items of which we have spoken, but underneath these sections was a third secret compartment. When this was opened, we found thirteen children who were barely alive."

Henrietta's mouth hits the floor. She is devastated. What was it Donal had said at the beginning: "takes them over a line of no return."

This has now happened. Henrietta cannot go on with this on her conscience. Even though she knew nothing previously of this; she has turned a blind eye to so many other situations and taken Bond's side even when she knew it was wrong, but this is definitely the straw that has broken the camel's back!

"I knew nothing of this" begins Henrietta, "and this changes the whole situation. I cannot stand by and say nothing of Councillor Bond's involvement in all of this."

Donal lets out a small sigh of satisfaction and hands Henrietta a statement to read, which has been prepared beforehand, and says:

"Please look over this and if you agree with all the facts, sign and initial each page. If there is anything else you wish to add, write your notes on the last page."

Henrietta needs three more pages to add other salient information and after reading through this, Donal begins to feel that they have a very strong case against Bond. There is another point that Henrietta has brought up on her additional pages which has Donal increasing his heartbeat and that is the name of Detective Rodney Bull.

It seems he is involved in supplying information of times and dates that have facilitated movements of many of the lorries. He and Bond had corresponded about certain compromising secrets that they knew about Commander Atkins. This could be the break that his chief has been after!

Chapter Sixteen

Shoot out at the Met

Chief Constable David Doyle has called a meeting with Commander Atkins, Detective Sergeant Donal Jones and Detective Constable Rodney Bull. The meeting is in the Chief Constable's offices at New Scotland Yard. David Doyle begins:

"Come in gentlemen and take a seat. I would like to outline the situation from my perspective and then listen to your comments."

After the Chief has been through the sequence of events from the finding of the counterfeiting equipment to the death of Thomas and the murder of Kurt, he turns to the Commander and asks if he has anything to add. Claude Atkins looks distinctly uncomfortable and shifts in his seat. For a man of his experience he seems very ill at ease with the situation. He begins:

"I am somewhat disappointed with Detective Bull's performance over the death of Thomas the Lithuanian as I'm sure, if he were alive, he could have given us far more information on the source of the counterfeiting. Having said that, I have had Bull working undercover on Councillor Bond for many months and this has now shed light on the involvement of Sir Charles Grimwall."

Donal couldn't contain himself any longer and launches in:

"With all due respect Commander I put it to you that far from instigating this enquiry you are in fact one of the main protagonists in this whole affair. We have reliable information that you have been blackmailed by Rodney Bull to protect the organisation from prosecution by the Met. I also accuse you Detective Bull of murdering the other Lithuanian, Kurt to stop him talking, especially as you failed to return to the station until the following morning even though you were specifically asked to do so forthwith. This would have given you plenty of time to visit the house where Kurt was staying and finish him off before returning."

All eyes were on Bull. Was his name apt for the explanation he was going to give, or could he convince them that he was indeed one of the good guys.

"This isn't some situation from an Agatha Christie novel Sergeant Jones that you can accuse me of with flimsy circumstantial evidence and expect me to just say: 'Fair cop Guv, you've got me bang to rights'. You have no hard evidence against me for the murder."

"Apart from myself and Harry O'Brien who never entered the house," replies Donal "no-one knew of Kurt's whereabouts. Also the weapon that killed him had been put back in a rack and wiped clean. All the other knives had fingerprints on them. This was clearly a professional job. Someone who knew the procedures that forensics would take and act accordingly without panic."

"We're going round in circles here," retorts Bull "you clearly don't have positive evidence against me, and how could I be blackmailing the Commander when he has put me in the frame?"

Bull looked at the Commander with an assured smirk on his face and thought to himself that although staying in the force was unlikely, he seemed to have covered his tracks regarding the murder.

"You're right that this is no Agatha Christie murder mystery," begins Donal "but you may wish it were when I reveal what forensics also found. In Kurt's right hand was a piece of cloth from a jacket very like the one you were wearing that night and on that piece of cloth were two sources of DNA. One was non human, probably a rodent, possibly a mouse and the other one was yours."

Bull's jaw drops. He's been beaten by that pesky rat. He slumps into his chair as Donal begins the formal words:

"Detective Constable Rodney Bull I am arresting you for the murder of etc.," after which David Doyle concludes the meeting and finishes by telling Commander Atkins that he will be investigated by the internal affairs commission.

When Atkins and Bull have been led away by officers who were waiting outside, the chief turns to Donal and says:

"Good work Detective...Inspector Jones and congratulations on your work and your new appointment. After this we can pick up Bond and I'll put out an international warrant for Alan Trask. I'm also organising a commendation for Harry O'Brien for the use of his boat and taking a substantial risk in following the suspect."

Chapter Seventeen

Celebration

Donal can't wait to get home and share the good news with Samantha and as soon as he's stopped off for a bottle of champagne for the fridge and a carrot and ginger smoothie for Jasmine, he's on his way.

"D'you want the good news or the bad news?" Donal starts as he almost runs into the hallway clutching the drinks. "Where's Jazz? I've got her favourite smoothie here."

"Where's the fire?" Exclaims Sam as she rushes in from the kitchen on hearing all the noise.

"We're going to celebrate!" Announces Donal, "the bad news is I'm going to be loud and excited all evening but the good news is that Jazz no longer has to worry about ex-Councillor Bond being around."

Jasmine runs down the stairs and gives her dad a welcome hug and they all sit down in the lounge and Donal fills them in on much of the detail, without saying too much that might prejudice the trial.

"The funny thing about the end of this" begins Donal, "is that both of the main events seemed to have been saved by the intervention of a rodent."

Donal hadn't given details of the murder, only that the mole in the police had been inadvertently caught out by a rat's actions.

"That's only half the truth" thinks Jasmine as she reflects on the mind reading act that she and her dad had performed at the annual Christmas do.

"Have we any crab sticks in the fridge?' Jazz asks.

"Yes there are" replies Sam, "but we'll eat soon so don't spoil your appetite."

"I won't" says Jazz, "but I need to text a couple of friends and that'll keep me going until the main event."

Without more ado Jazz bounds out of the room, takes a couple of crab sticks from the fridge and runs back upstairs where she knows Reggie is waiting.

Reggie has enjoyed his early evening with Jasmine and especially those crab sticks, but is secretly pleased when she needs to have a celebratory meal with her folks downstairs. Pam Potts is having a flat leaving party before she moves to her new house in Maple Walk and Reggie knows that Lucy will be there with her new partner Leroy.

"It's always the same" thinks Reggie, "parties are like buses; none for ages, then they all come at once!"

Pam has invited Percy and many of her neighbours whom she's known for over twenty years. It is going to be a noisy affair but Pam has made provision on her small balcony for all of Lucy's friends so they can enjoy the revelry too. Ollie and all his brood are perched on the balcony rail along with Lucy and Leroy and a host of the rodent population that have known Reggie for many years.

Pam keeps the door to the balcony closed for most of the time except when throwing out scraps and tit bits for the ensemble as she knows some of the neighbours may not share her appreciation of some of her 'pets'.

However from time to time Rose Almond pops out to see them all and shares some memories of Ollie's escape back to the country.

Chapter Eighteen

Epilogue

Reggie feels very tired. He is thirteen which in human years (eight rat years to a human one) equates to a hundred and four. No wonder he feels tired! After all his exertions and having had the best day of his life, he feels as though he could sleep for a week. After what seems like an age he manages to struggle along the beach to the O'Brien's abode; his second home. As he reaches the patio doors overlooking the sea, he can see Clair sitting on the sofa quietly reading.

"Hello Reggie, come up here on the sofa" says Clair and Reggie doesn't need asking twice. He lays his head on Clair's lap and for the first time in his life feels at peace with the world. He can remember Clair once talking to Harry about reincarnation and that if you have had a good life and have respected others around you, it is possible to come back on a higher level of the food chain.

"I'd like to come back as an owl" he muses, "they seem very wise and I have many friends who are owls."

Just then Harry 'O' comes in and Reggie struggles to sit up.

"Hello old friend" says Harry, "don't get up on my account, I'm just here to make Clair a drink."

"Thanks Harry" replies Clair, "I'd love a hot chocolate."

As Clair is talking, she looks at Harry with a knowing expression and then glances down at Reggie and strokes his back. Both of them sense that he is near the end. Reggie closes his eyes, snuggles further down by Clair's side and drifts off into an amazing sleep.

Pam Potts has just moved to Maple Walk and taken in a refugee child. She doesn't know exactly where he comes from as his skin is brown but he speaks English with a slight Sussex accent. Pam is pleased to foster him in her new home and she's glad of the company. She estimates he must be around thirteen or fourteen years old.

Sam has asked Jasmine to call in with a cake and a bottle of wine to welcome Pam to their road and so Jasmine knocks on the door.

"Oh Jasmine it's lovely to see you, what can I do for you?" She ventures as she opens the door.

"I've just come to welcome you to our Walk and please accept these as a housewarming present" says Jasmine handing the gifts to Pam.

"Oh that's so kind of you, please come in and share a slice of cake. You can meet my new foster child."

Jasmine steps over the threshold into the hallway and sees a figure standing by the door to the kitchen.

"Jasmine I'd like you to meet Reggie Ratner, Reggie this is Jasmine Jones, a lovely neighbour."

Reggie and Jasmine stare at each other. Neither can catch a breath. They both hesitantly walk towards each other, Reggie extending a hand to shake Jasmine's, but she cannot contain herself and surges forward to embrace Reggie before she has time to think.

"It's wonderful to meet you" says Reggie as he returns Jasmine's hug, and as their heads turn to either side of the embrace, he finds his nose has gently nuzzled into Jasmine's neck.